Karen's Big Top

Look for these
and other books about Karen
in the
Baby-sitters Little Sister series:

Little Sister

Karen's Big Top
Ann M. Martin

Illustrations by Susan Tang

A
LITTLE APPLE
PAPERBACK

SCHOLASTIC INC.
New York Toronto London Auckland Sydney

ISBN 0-590-48229-7

12 11 10 9 8 7 6 5 4 3   5 6 7 8 9/9

Printed in the U.S.A.   40

First Scholastic printing, July 1994

The author gratefully acknowledges
Stephanie Calmenson
for her help
with this book.

Karen's Big Top

Circus Camp

Y-A-W-N. S-T-R-E-T-C-H.

"Good morning, Goosie," I said to my stuffed cat.

"Good morning, Emily," I said to my pet rat.

It was a Monday morning at the end of June. But I did not have to get up to go to school. It was summer vacation. I could sleep all day long.

I did not want to sleep. There was too much to do.

I tumbled out of my bed. In case you are

wondering why I did not climb out of bed like everyone else, I will tell you. In one week I am going to circus camp. I just know that circus performers do not climb out of places. They tumble.

"Karen!" called Mommy. "Would you like some breakfast?"

"I'm on my way!" I replied.

My name is Karen Brewer. I am seven years old. I have blonde hair, blue eyes, and some freckles. Oh, yes. I wear glasses. I even have two pairs. I have a blue pair for reading. And I have a pink pair for the rest of the time.

While I am getting dressed, I will tell you about the circus camp. It is called the B. F. Willie Big Top. Mr. B. F. Willie and his family run the camp right here in Stoneybrook, where I live.

The Willies are a real and true circus family. Most of the time, they travel around the country performing. But every year for the whole month of July, Mr. Willie likes to come to Stoneybrook. That is because he grew up here. He takes a break from traveling and performing to teach kids about being in the circus.

I was finished dressing. I looked at myself in the mirror. I was wearing red sandals, green socks, blue shorts, a pink T-shirt, and purple barrettes in my hair. Not one thing matched.

"That's okay, Goosie," I said. "My clothes are funny. Maybe I will be a circus clown."

I ran downstairs to have my breakfast.

"Hi, Mommy! Hi, Andrew!" I said.

(Andrew is my little brother. He is four going on five. He is too little to go to circus camp.)

"Hey, Karen, you have on a lot of colors," said Andrew. "I can name them. Red, green, blue, poiple . . ."

I ate my bowl of Krispie Krunchy cereal and drank my glass of apple juice in record time.

"May I go out and play with Nancy now?" I asked.

"Of course," said Mommy.

Nancy and I had a lot to talk about. You see, I am not going to circus camp by myself. I am going with my two best friends, Nancy Dawes and Hannie Papadakis. We call ourselves the Three Musketeers. That is because we do almost everything together.

I started walking toward Nancy's house. Guess what! Nancy was walking toward me.

"I was just coming to find you," she said.

"I was just coming to find *you*," I replied.

Nancy looked at my clothes. She made a funny face. I could tell she was trying hard not to laugh.

"It's okay," I said. "I know I look like a clown. Hey, let's both be clowns. Clowns-for-the-day!"

"That is a great idea!" said Nancy. "I will ask my mother if we can use her makeup."

"And I have a box of funny clothes in my closet," I said.

We raced back to my house. My little

house that is. I have another house, too. It is my big house. I am going to live there in July. There are so many people living in my big house, it is like a circus. That means I will live in a circus house and go to a circus camp.

July is going to be very exciting.

2

The Big-House Month

I will tell you how I got to have two houses. When I was little, I only had one. I lived in the big house with Daddy, Mommy, and Andrew. But then Daddy and Mommy started fighting a lot. They explained to Andrew and me that they still loved us very much. But they did not want to be married to each other anymore. So they got a divorce.

Mommy moved with Andrew and me into the little house. She got married again to a man named Seth Engle. That makes him my stepfather. This is who lives at the little house: Mommy, Seth, Andrew, me, Midgie (Seth's dog), Rocky (Seth's cat), Emily Junior (my rat), and Bob (Andrew's hermit crab).

Andrew and I live in the little house with Mommy for one month. Then we live in the big house with Daddy the next month. Both houses are in Stoneybrook, Connecticut.

Even when we are not at the big house, Daddy has lots of company. That is because after the divorce, he married Elizabeth Thomas. That makes her my stepmother. She was married before and had four children. They are Kristy, who is thirteen and the best stepsister ever; Sam and Charlie, who are so old they are in high school; and David Michael, who is seven, but an older seven than me.

Then Daddy and Elizabeth adopted Emily Michelle from a faraway place called Vietnam. She is two and a half. (I named my pet rat after her.)

Nannie, Elizabeth's mother, came to live at the big house to help take care of Emily Michelle. But really she helps take care of everyone. Nannie is a gigundoly wonderful stepgrandmother.

Are you ready to hear about the pets at the big house? They are Boo-Boo, who is Daddy's mean old cat; Shannon, who is David Michael's very big puppy; Crystal Light and Goldfishie, who are you-know-whats; and Emily Junior and Bob, who go wherever Andrew and I go.

I have special names for Andrew and me. I call us Andrew Two-Two and Karen Two-Two. (I got the idea for those names from a book my teacher read at school. It was called, *Jacob Two-Two Meets the Hooded Fang*.) The reason I call us two-twos is because we have two of so many different things. We have two houses. We have two sets of clothes and toys and books. I have two stuffed cats. (Goosie is my little-house cat. Moosie is my big-house cat.) I have two pieces of Tickly, my special blanket. And of course, I have my two best friends. Nancy lives next door to Mommy's house and Hannie lives across the street and one house down from Daddy's house. Having two of everything makes it easier to move back and forth every month.

Being a two-two is not always easy, though. Sometimes I miss Mommy. And sometimes I miss Daddy. And even though I have two of lots of things, somehow I still leave a thing or two at the wrong house.

But most of the time being a two-two is just fine. There are people and animals all around. And there is always something going on. It really is like the circus. Step right up to the Brewer-Thomas Big Top!

Fireworks

" 'Bye, Mommy! See you in August!" I called.

"Have fun, kids. Love you!" said Mommy.

It was Thursday, the first day of July. Andrew and I were moving to the big house for a month. We had had fun at the little house in June. Now we were ready for some big-house fun.

Circus camp did not start until Monday. That meant four free days to do anything I wanted.

10

"Hi, kids!" called Daddy. He was waiting for us at the door. He scooped us up in big hugs.

"Are you ready for lunch?" he asked. "While we eat, we are going to make plans for Sunday."

"What's on Sunday?" asked Andrew.

I had to think for a minute. Then I remembered.

"It is the Fourth of July!" I cried.

I dropped my things and raced into the kitchen.

"Hi," said Kristy. "We're glad you're here. We did not want to make any holiday plans without you."

(I told you Kristy was the best stepsister ever.)

We agreed to have an afternoon barbecue with our neighbors. At night, we would listen to an outdoor concert and watch the fireworks.

I could hardly wait. I counted down the days.

When I woke up on Sunday, I ran from

room to room calling, "Happy Fourth of July!"

"You sound like a Fourth of July fire-cracker," said Elizabeth. She was holding her ears and smiling.

Guess what. Daddy got permission from the police to close our block to traffic. We held the barbecue right in the middle of the street. Everyone who lived on the block was there.

"Who wants to have a hot dog-eating contest?" I asked.

Here is who entered the contest: David Michael, Hannie and her brother Linny, Melody and Bill Korman, Maria Kilbourne, Scott Hsu.

Sam was the judge. He put out a big plate of hot dogs.

"On your mark, get set, eat!" he called.

After three and a half hot dogs, I was stuffed. Instead of eating, I started barking like a dog. A hot dog!

"Woof! Woof-woof!" I said.

"Arf!" answered Hannie.

"Grrr!" growled David Michael.

We forgot about the contest. We were too busy barking, growling, and howling.

After the barbecue we piled into cars and headed for Stoneybrook University for the outdoor concert. They played songs like "Yankee Doodle Dandy" and "The Star-Spangled Banner."

As soon as it got dark, the fireworks started. They were gigundoly beautiful! First, a big red and orange star exploded in the sky. Just as it was disappearing, I heard a whistling in the air. Another rocket was flying up. It burst into blues and greens and fell like glitter all around.

"Yipee!" I shouted every time the sky lit up.

When the fireworks were over, I was ready to go home. I was tired. It had been a big day, even for me.

"Psst," whispered Kristy when we got back to the big house. "In here."

Everyone except Daddy, Elizabeth, Nannie, and Emily Michelle followed Kristy into

14

the kitchen. (They had already gone upstairs.)

"Listen, Nannie's birthday is at the end of July. We should plan something special for her," said Kristy. "I know it is late now. We do not have to decide what to do tonight. Just think of things that would be nice."

I had a lot to think about when I got into bed. Nannie's birthday. And circus camp. Tomorrow was my first day.

I meant to think about both of these things. I really did. But as soon as my head hit the pillow, I was fast asleep.

4

B. F. Willie

"Is it time to go? Is it time?" I asked.

"It's time," said Charlie.

It was early Monday morning. Hannie had come to the big house to have breakfast with me.

Charlie was driving us to camp on our first day. The camp was all the way out at the edge of town.

On the way, Hannie and I tried to guess what the "B. F." in B. F. Willie stood for. Butterfly? Baby face? Big foot?

"I know!" I cried. "He is Big Fat Willie,

the fat man at the circus. I can hear his big fat footsteps now. *Stomp. Stomp.* They are getting closer. And closer. And . . ."

"And we're here," announced Charlie.

He pulled up to a line of trailers. Behind the trailers was a tent with a banner that said THE B. F. WILLIE BIG TOP.

"There's Nancy," said Hannie.

We said good-bye to Charlie and raced up to meet her. A girl who looked about Kristy's age came up to us.

"Hi," she said. "I'm Laura Willie. Mr. Willie is my uncle. He asked me to help greet some of the campers."

Laura showed us where to put our lunch and our change of clothes. Then she led us to a meeting area where all the campers were gathering. The youngest campers were around six. The oldest looked around twelve.

"Hi, Karen," called a familiar voice.

It was Ricky Torres. Natalie Springer was there too. They are both in my class at school.

When it looked like the last of the campers had arrived, a man climbed up on a platform to talk to us.

"Good morning," he said. "I am Mr. B. F. Willie."

"He is not big and fat at all," I whispered.

Mr. Willie looked a lot older than Daddy. His hair was gray, and his skin was wrinkled. But he looked strong and fit. And he had a friendly smile.

"While you are here, we will teach you as much about being in a circus as we can. As you can see, I am no spring chicken," Mr. Willie said, flapping his arms like a chicken. "But I still perform in every show. I hope you will grow to love the circus as much as I do."

He introduced us to his family. They were his wife, sisters, brothers, nieces, nephews, and grandchildren.

"And that's not all. Every circus member is a member of the B. F. Willie family. For the month of July, that includes every one of you."

18

Wow! His family was bigger than mine!

I hoped I would get to talk to his grand-daughter, Jillian. She was eight. I had a lot of questions to ask her about life in a traveling circus.

"And now for the grand tour," said Mr. Willie.

He led us into a big circus tent and showed us all the equipment. The trapeze. The trampoline. The clown car.

"Can you believe it," I said. "We are in the middle of a real live circus."

"Look, there are horses out back," said Hannie.

The horses were grazing in a field. When Jillian saw us looking at them, she came over.

"Aren't they pretty? We have lots of animals here," she said. "I love all animals. I help take care of them."

"Maybe I could help too. I have a pet rat named Emily. I take very good care of her," I said.

"Great," said Jillian.

I wondered if Jillian got to ride the horses. I wondered how she could go to school if she was traveling all the time. I wondered if she had a best friend. I would have to ask her all these important questions.

We took a break for lunch, then changed into our tumbling clothes.

"One, two, three, over!" called Laura.

I did a stupendous backward somersault. Then I stood up and took a bow. And another bow. And another.

Wait till I told my big-house family about my first day at camp!

5

The High Wire

On Tuesday morning, Mr. Willie broke us up into groups of five. Every day the groups would work on a different stunt.

Ricky was in my group. (I was glad because Ricky is my pretend husband. We were married on the playground at school one day. It is good for married people to do interesting things together.)

Jimmy, Laura's older brother, was in charge of our group.

"Today we are going to learn about walking on the high wire," said Jimmy. "We will — "

"Yipee! I *love* the high wire," I cried. "It is the best thing at the circus."

"I am glad you are happy, Karen," said Jimmy. (I wondered how Jimmy knew my name. Then I remembered we were wearing name tags.)

"We will use this practice rope and net to learn how to balance and how to fall. As you can see, the rope is not as high as a real high wire. But you use the same skills to walk across it," said Jimmy. "Who will take the first turn?"

"I will! I will!" I cried.

"I knew I could count on you, Karen," said Jimmy, smiling.

I took off my sneakers and socks and climbed up the ladder. Jimmy showed me how to place my feet on the rope. He gave me a long rod to hold in front of me.

"This will help you to balance," he said.

I was not scared at all. That is because I have taken gymnastics. My teacher, Miss

Donovan, said my balance was very good. I had to concentrate. But I walked right across the rope without even wobbling.

"That was great, Karen," said Jimmy.

"But I did not get to fall," I said.

"We will practice that later on. Ricky, why don't you take the next turn," said Jimmy.

Ricky went across the rope, just like I did. I was very proud of my pretend husband. Only one of the kids, Robin, was a little bit scared. But Jimmy held her hand and she went across, too.

When everyone had a turn walking the rope, we climbed back up and jumped down into the net. That was my favorite part.

"Good work, kids," said Jimmy. "Now it is time for lunch. This afternoon, we will not break up into our groups. We will have a surprise for you instead."

Here is what the surprise turned out to be. The B. F. Willie Big Top put on a show just for us.

"I want you to see us perform some of the acts from our circus," said Mr. Willie. "That way, you will know what you are working toward."

Mr. Willie began the show by doing a trapeze act with Mrs. Willie. Mrs. Willie went flying through the air. Mr. Willie caught her just before the trapeze swung away.

Jimmy and Laura did a juggling act. While they were juggling, Jillian came out riding her pony. She was standing up on the pony's back.

Then she did bareback acrobatics. First she did a handstand. Then she did a backward somersault and landed on her horse again.

She finished by jumping down and juggling with Jimmy and Laura.

Jillian could do so many things. She must have worked very hard to learn them. I wondered if she practiced all day long.

I hoped I would get to talk to her soon.

6

A Surprise Party
for Nannie

I walked into the big house making believe
I was on the high wire. I held my arms out
at my sides and carefully stepped into the
living room.

"Oh, my goodness. Look at this daring
feat," said Elizabeth.

I wobbled a little to make everyone nervous. When I got near the couch, I jumped
off the make-believe wire.

"Bravo!" called Daddy. "I hope this
means you had a good time at circus
camp."

26

"It was the greatest!" I said.

"Come tell us all about it at dinner," said Elizabeth.

We were having ravioli, salad, and bread. Between bites, I told my big-house family all about my day at camp. I did not leave one thing out.

Then I called Mommy and Seth. I told the whole story over again.

When I hung up, Kristy was waiting for me.

"Karen, will you come up to my room for a minute?" she whispered. "We need to have a meeting."

Charlie, Sam, David Michael, and Andrew were already there. (Emily Michelle was not there. She is still too little for important meetings.)

"I thought it would be good to toss around some ideas for Nannie's birthday celebration," said Kristy. "Does anyone have any suggestions?"

"I have an idea," said David Michael. "We could put on a show for Nannie."

(David Michael was a Winkie in *The Wizard of Oz*. He loves putting on shows.)

"That's a nice idea," said Charlie. "But we're all so busy this summer. I don't think we would have time to rehearse."

"How about taking Nannie out shopping?" said Sam. "We could buy her anything she wants."

"You know Nannie," said Kristy. "She'll tell us she doesn't need anything."

"Why don't we give her a big party. It could even be a surprise party!" I said.

"That's a great idea, Karen," said Kristy. "That will make Nannie feel really special."

"And it is something we can all do together," said Charlie. "Each of us will have a different job. Even Emily Michelle can help."

"Maybe we'd better see what Daddy and Elizabeth think first," I suggested.

"I'll go find them," said Kristy.

She brought Daddy and Elizabeth back to the room. We told them our idea.

"That sounds like a wonderful plan,"

said Elizabeth. "I think Nannie will love it."

"I agree," said Daddy. "We'll have to be very careful about keeping the secret. Do you all think you can do it?"

I could tell Daddy was looking my way. Sometimes I am not very good with secrets. I get excited and blurt them out.

"I will be very careful and keep the secret," I promised.

"Me too," said David Michael.

We all took turns promising to keep Nannie's surprise party secret.

"I will not tell. I will not tell," I said to Moosie when I got into bed.

When I fell asleep, I dreamed it was Nannie's birthday. She was very happy with her surprise. The party was at the B. F. Willie Big Top. Nannie took a turn walking the high wire. She jumped up and twirled in the air.

Way to go, Nannie!

The Flying Trapeze

On Wednesday morning I said good-bye to Hannie and Nancy and went to find my group. Every day we learn something new at circus camp. I wondered what we would be learning today.

"Over here," called Jimmy. He was at the trampoline.

"Wow! I *love* the trampoline," I said.

"I thought you might say that," said Jimmy, laughing.

"Hi, Karen," said Jillian. "I am going to be one of the spotters today."

"I hope you will not have to catch me," I said.

"I am sure I will not have to. I have been watching you. You are very good at everything," said Jillian.

I really was good on the trampoline. I bounced way up in the air. Then Jimmy helped me do a forward somersault.

When it was time for lunch, I invited Jillian to join the Three Musketeers.

"Thanks," said Jillian. "I'll go get my sandwich and come right back."

We sat on a bench outside. While we were eating, I asked Jillian some of my questions.

"How do you go to school if you are traveling all the time?" I asked.

"I have a tutor. We study a few hours in the morning and again in the afternoon," said Jillian.

"That is neat. I wish I had my own personal tutor. We have one teacher for a whole class of kids," I said.

"We're in the same class at school," said Hannie.

"You're lucky. Sometimes I wonder what it would be like to live in one place and go to a real school like other kids," said Jillian.

"Do you get to play with the elephants much?" asked Nancy.

"Sure, I play with them. But I have to take care of them too. I feed and clean and exercise all the animals," said Jillian.

Having so many animals sounded like fun.

"I only have my one rat," I said.

"But it is your very own. I have to share the animals with everyone in the circus," said Jillian.

After lunch, we went back to our groups.

"Mr. Willie is going to give us a lesson on the trapeze this afternoon," said Jimmy. "But do not worry. You will be wearing safety harnesses, so you cannot fall."

Jimmy looked at me. "Aren't you going to say something?" he asked.

"Oh, right. I almost forgot. I *love* the trapeze!" I shouted.

When my turn came, Jimmy put the harness around my waist. I climbed up a ladder and stepped out onto a platform. Mr. Willie was there waiting for me. He hooked ropes to the harness. Then he helped me grab the swing. I hung on and went sailing through the air like a bird.

"Hello down there," I called. But I knew no one could hear me.

On Thursday, we had acrobatics in the morning, and juggling in the afternoon. I *love* acrobatics! I *love* juggling!

Jillian helped our group both times. And she had lunch again with the Three Musketeers.

Jillian was nice. She answered all my questions about being in a traveling circus. And I answered her questions about life in Stoneybrook.

Guess whose life sounded more exciting.

Karen Brewer,
Circus Star

"Good morning, circus performers," said Mr. Willie. "Welcome to the last day of your first week. You have all been doing a great job so far."

It was Friday. I could not believe our first week was almost over. Circus camp was going too fast.

"Now that you have had a taste of circus life, I want to tell you our plan for the rest of the month," said Mr. Willie. "For the next two weeks, you will continue working on your circus skills. I would like you to think about the one thing you like the best. You will be asked to practice only that thing the last week you are here. On the Saturday after camp ends, you will put on your own circus show for your families.''

I was going to be in a circus! Of course I would be the star. I could see the banner now:

The B. F. Willie Big Top
presents
KAREN BREWER, CIRCUS STAR

Everyone would come to see me. Mommy and Seth and my whole big-house family. (I was sure Emily Junior would want to come. I wondered if they would let a pet rat into the circus.)

Now, what would I do at the circus. Fly on the trapeze? Be a funny clown? Ride bareback on my beautiful horse?

I could not decide. All I knew was that I would be wearing a costume that was very

sparkly and spangly. And it would have a
great big feather.

"Karen! Earth to Karen!" called Jimmy.

My group was way over at the other side
of the tent. It looked like Hannie and Nancy's group was there too.

"Coming!" I called.

I ran over to see what we were going to
do. I did not want to miss a minute of my
circus training.

"You are going to be the first two groups
to learn about making costumes," said
Jimmy.

"Yipee!" I cried.

"I am glad the Three Musketeers can
make costumes together," said Nancy.

"Laura and I will show you a few of the
costumes that we use. Then we will get
your ideas for the kinds of costumes you
would like to see," said Jimmy.

"Here is the costume that the sword
swallower wears," said Laura.

"Ooh, it is dangly and spangly!" I said.

The pants were red with gold fringes

dangling down from the sides. There was a white shirt with ruffles all the way down the front. And there was a spangly vest with sequins and tassels all over it.

"This is what the jugglers wear," said Jimmy.

The tops were red and silky. The bottoms were black satin with velvet trim.

We saw many beautiful costumes. Then Jimmy asked for our ideas.

"If I were the sword swallower, I would want to wear a red cape," said Ricky.

"That sounds good," said Laura. "I would like you and all the boys to buy or make capes and bring them to our third week of camp."

"What about feathers?" I asked. "These costumes really should have feathers, you know."

"I think you are right, Karen. Feathers would be perfect," said Jimmy. "It would be great if you could bring some in. We would also like each of the girls to bring in a leotard."

"You will each make the costume you are going to wear when you perform for your families," said Laura.

Feathers. Leotard. Oh, yes. Some sparkly sequins, too.

I was going to be a gigundoly beautiful circus star.

9

The Bowling Party

It was Sunday morning. I was in the yard teaching Andrew how to tumble.

"One, two, three, over!" I said.

Andrew rolled over on his side like a bug.

"Like that?" asked Andrew.

"I think we'd better try it again," I replied.

Just then Kristy poked her head out the door.

"Important meeting," she said. "My room."

Andrew and I followed Kristy upstairs. David Michael, Sam, and Charlie were already there.

"We have to make some decisions today," said Kristy. "We need to decide what to buy, what to serve, and who to invite. You give me your ideas. I will write them down."

Here is what went on Kristy's list:

Decorations: streamers, balloons, confetti

Presents: sweater, book, movie tickets

Food: pizza, green salad, soda, juice, birthday cake

Guests: Elizabeth, Watson, Emily Michelle, all of us, Nannie's friends (get list from Elizabeth)

"Now comes the hard part," said Kristy. "How will we surprise Nannie?"

Andrew raised his hand.

"We could tell Nannie to get dressed up and meet us in the living room," he said.

"I think we will have to be a little trick-ier," said Charlie.

"I have a tricky idea," I said. "I will have Hannie call me on the phone. I will say things like 'Oh, no!' and 'It cannot be!' Then I will tell Nannie that one of the circus el-ephants got loose. I will ask her to help me find it. Nannie will take me out riding in the neighborhood and . . ."

"I think that may be a little *too* tricky," said Sam.

"I will tell Nannie I cannot get my fingers out of her bowling ball. We will have to go to the doctor to get me unstuck," said David Michael.

"Hmm. That gives me an idea," said Kristy. "Nannie loves her bowling team. They should be part of our surprise."

"Maybe they could take her out to dinner for her birthday. They can bring her to the bowling alley afterward for a birthday bowl-ing game. And we will be waiting there to surprise her!" I said.

42

(I tried to talk very quietly. I did not want to let Nannie hear our secret plans.)

"Hey, that's not bad. Do you really think we could have our party at the bowling alley?" said Sam.

"Why not?" replied Charlie. "After we have eaten and Nannie has opened her presents, everyone can bowl."

"It's a great idea," said Kristy. "I cannot think of anything Nannie would like better than a bowling party."

We decided to call the bowling alley to see how much it would cost to have the party there. We would have to ask Daddy and Elizabeth if they would pay for that part of the party.

"I'll call one of Nannie's teammates," said Kristy. "I am sure her friends will want to be part of the surprise."

"This plan is great. When the Brewer-Thomas kids need to get something done, watch out!" I said.

"Please just watch out that you don't

give away the secret," said Charlie.

"You do not have to worry about me," I said.

I closed my mouth and pulled my fingers across my lips. Then I made believe I was throwing away a key.

I wanted everyone to see that my lips were sealed.

Lulu

"*H*onk, *honk!*" I squeezed my red rubber clown nose.

It was fun to be a clown! It was my new favorite thing to be at the circus.

It was Wednesday. It was my second week at camp.

On Monday, my favorite thing was the flying trapeze. I can do stunts.

On Tuesday my favorite thing was the trampoline. I can twirl in the air.

"Karen, do you want to help me take care of the animals today? Grandpa said it would be okay," said Jillian.

"Sure," I said. "What should we do first?"

I was ready for anything. Taming lions. Swinging from an elephant's trunk. I could be a world-famous animal trainer.

"Let's clean the elephant stalls first," said Jillian.

"Yuck. Maybe I should help you later," I said.

"Come on, Karen," said Jillian. "It's not so bad."

It was pretty bad at first. Mostly it was smelly. But I got used to it. When we finished, the elephants looked very grateful. (Their names were Henry, Sophie, and Lilly. They are gigundoly graceful dancers.)

"Now Monty gets a bath," said Jillian.

Monty is a white poodle. He jumps through hoops. Sometimes he rolls in mud. Then he is a gray poodle.

We put Monty in a tub of warm water. I put on the shampoo. I was careful not to get any near his eyes.

"We need towels," said Jillian. "I will be right back."

I was rubbing shampoo into Monty's coat when Natalie passed by. She had on a clown nose. *Honk! Honk!*

Monty thought it was a toy. He jumped out of the tub. He ran after Natalie. Natalie ran the other way.

"Monty, come back here!" I cried. He kept running.

"Monty," called Jillian. Monty looked her way.

Jillian lifted her arm straight up in the air. Monty dropped down to the ground and did not move.

"Wow. Monty knows sign language," I said.

"I did the sign for *down*. I can teach you the signs. Then Monty will obey you, too," said Jillian.

We finished Monty's bath. Then we put him in his crate to rest. He liked his crate. It was cozy. He had a rug, toys, and fresh water in case he got thirsty.

Jillian looked at her watch.

"I guess you will not get to groom Lulu today. It is almost time to go home," she said.

Lulu was the white pony Jillian rode in the circus show. I wanted to groom her. I wanted to ride her!

"Hi, Karen," said Hannie. "My mom called Mr. Willie to say she was going to pick us up a little late."

"Hmm. I have an idea," said Jillian. "I just have to ask Grandpa if it is okay."

In a little while, Jillian came back. Jimmy was with her. By then, all the other kids had gone home.

"Okay," said Jillian, smiling. "Who wants to ride first?"

"Ride? We are going to ride Lulu?" I cried.

Lulu jumped back a few steps.

"It is a good idea not to shout in Lulu's ear. She gets a little spooked," said Jimmy.

"Sorry," I whispered to Lulu. I patted her nose.

48

"Karen, you can go first since you helped with the animals today," said Jimmy. "Come on. I will help you up."

Jimmy cupped his hands. I stepped up and climbed onto Lulu's back. Jillian held the reins and led me around the circus ring. Then she let go.

"How does it feel to be a bareback rider at the circus?" called Jimmy.

"It is the greatest!" I said.

I smiled and waved to my adoring fans.

Eavesdropping

"What could we do that would be fun, Moosie?" I asked.

Moosie did not answer. He was taking a cat nap.

It was Friday night at the big house. I had nothing to do. And there was no one to do nothing with.

Kristy was baby-sitting. Sam and Charlie were out with their friends. David Michael would not look up from the book he was reading.

Maybe I will go catch fireflies in the yard,

I thought. That will be fun.

I looked out the window. Boo and bull-frogs. It was raining.

I got another idea right away. It would be breaking a big-house rule. The rule is: No spying allowed. But spying is so much fun. I decided to break the rule. Just this once.

Who could I spy on? Emily Michelle was asleep. Daddy and Elizabeth were paying bills. Nannie was . . .

Hey, where was Nannie? I walked down the hall to see if Nannie was in her room.

Ring. Ring. It was Nannie's phone. I wondered if she was there.

"Hello," I heard Nannie say.

Goody. I can eavesdrop. I could not remember if there was a rule about eavesdropping. I was sure there was. Eavesdropping was spying, only with your ears. But I was going to do it just this once . . .

"I hear Gracie has a terrible cold," said

Nannie. "I told her to drink plenty of juice and take vitamin C."

Ho hum. This was not a very exciting conversation. I waited for Nannie to say something else. She didn't for the longest time. I guess the other person was talking a lot.

"Yes, my birthday is coming up soon," said Nannie.

Here we go! Something interesting. I pressed my ear to the door. I did not want to miss a word.

"I don't know if my family has anything planned. They haven't said so. I certainly hope they are not thinking of giving me a surprise party. I do not like surprises. I do not like being the center of attention. I would never know how to act if someone yelled 'surprise' at me. That would be awful," said Nannie.

Did she say awful? Uh-oh. My stomach did a flip-flop. I stepped back from the door. I had to do something. I had to tell someone.

I ran toward David Michael's room. But I stopped before I reached the door.

I cannot tell David Michael, I thought. I cannot tell anyone that Nannie does not like surprise parties. They will ask me how I know. I will have to tell them I was eavesdropping. I will get into big trouble.

I hurried back to my room.

"Moosie. Wake up," I said. "Nannie does not want a surprise party. She said it would be awful. I cannot tell anyone because I found out when I was eavesdropping. But I want to tell everyone we cannot have the party. It will embarrass Nannie."

Moosie just stared. He was not being very helpful tonight. I decided there was nothing I could do. At least not yet.

Karen's Tutu

"See you later, Charlie," I said.

Charlie dropped Hannie and Nancy and me at the entrance to camp. (The Three Musketeers had had a sleepover at the big house on Sunday night.)

Mr. Willie was waiting for the campers to arrive. When we were all there, he hopped up onto his platform.

"Good morning, circus performers. Welcome to your third week of camp," he said. "I want to remind you that our show is less than two weeks away. You should be thinking about what you would like to do in the show. I will be coming around to talk with each group later."

Mr. Willie did a forward somersault off the platform just for fun.

"Enjoy the day!" he said.

My group was going to work on costumes with Hannie and Nancy's group. I knew I would enjoy that.

"Did everyone remember to bring a leotard or cape?" asked Laura.

"Yes!!!" we all shouted.

I pulled my leotard out of my knapsack and waved it in the air. It was hot pink. (I had not found the perfect feather yet. But I would.)

"Help yourselves to any materials you need," said Jimmy. He pointed to a long table. There were plastic containers filled with all kinds of great stuff. I headed for the sparkly sequins.

I had a gigundoly brilliant plan for my tutu. (Is tutu the right word? I hoped so. I like it.) Anyway, here is my plan. I am going to put a border of all different colored sequins on my tutu. That will make it very sparkly. I will put stripes of sequins all down the sides. On the front of my leotard I will put a big K. K is for Karen in case you were wondering. (I had not decided where to put my feather yet.)

While the other kids were working, they were talking about the show.

"I want to be one of the jugglers," said Ricky. "I even practice at home. I am getting pretty good."

"I want to be on the trapeze," said Nancy. "I love being way up high."

I did not have time to think about what I would *do*. I was too busy thinking about how I would *look*.

I had an important decision to make about my costume. When I took my bows, there might be people in front *and* behind me. Should I put another K on the back of my tutu? I was trying to decide when Mr. Willie came over.

"I hope you have been thinking about

the show," he reminded the group. "You will need to make your choices soon, so we can plan the program."

Uh-oh. I did not want to be left out of the program. I'd better do some thinking after all.

"I like your sequins, Karen," said Jimmy when Mr. Willie had gone. "By the way, have you decided what you want to do in the show?"

"Um, I think I am going to be a juggler with Ricky," I said.

"That sounds good," said Jimmy.

"On second thought, I will go on the trapeze with Nancy. I like being up high, too," I said.

"Another good choice," said Jimmy.

"Wait! I really like Monty the poodle. And Jillian is teaching me hand signs. Maybe I will be one of the dog trainers."

"All right," said Jimmy.

"I take it back! I love riding Lulu. I want

to ride her bareback in the circus," I said. "Unless I decide to be a plate spinner."

"I guess you have a little more thinking to do," said Jimmy.

"I guess you are right," I replied.

13

Talking with Jillian

Guess what. Daddy and Elizabeth said I could stay late to play with Jillian.

"What should we do?" I asked. "Do you want to play circus? We can pretend we are circus stars together."

"That does not sound like so much fun to me. I am in the circus all the time. Let's play house instead," said Jillian. "We can pretend we are having friends over for tea."

"That does not sound so exciting to me. I do that all the time," I replied. "Do you want to take Lulu for a walk? You told me she needs to get a lot of exercise."

"Okay. She will like that," said Jillian.

We walked Lulu around the grounds a couple of times. We found a bale of hay out back. While Lulu ate, we sat on the top and talked.

"Tell me again about living in the big house. It sounds like so much fun," said Jillian.

"It is fun. Most of the time. Right now we are planning a surprise birthday party for Nannie. We will have it at the bowling alley. All her friends will be there," I said.

"I bet Nannie will love it," said Jillian.

"I am not so sure," I replied.

"Why not?" asked Jillian.

"Can you keep a secret?" I asked.

Jillian nodded.

I decided to tell about eavesdropping on Nannie. I knew my story would be safe with Jillian. I told her everything.

"So I know that a surprise party would be just awful," I said.

"When is the party?" asked Jillian.

"In a week. It is all planned," I replied.

"Boy, you'd better do something," said Jillian.

"I know. But what?" I asked.

"Talk to your grandmother," Jillian said.

"Talk to Nannie? I cannot do that. It would ruin the surprise. I promised everyone I would not give away the secret. They are all teasing me because they think I will. I just cannot spill the beans," I said.

"Well, you will get in trouble if you tell anyone else," said Jillian. "But your grandmother will be glad you told."

"But what about the surprise?" I asked. "What will we do about the party?"

"I am not sure," said Jillian. "But I think you should tell your grandmother no matter what."

"Maybe you are right. I will have to think about it," I replied.

Just then, I saw Elizabeth's car pulling up to the circus. She got out and waved to me.

"I have to go," I said.

I climbed down from the haystack and

headed for the car. Then I turned back. I had an idea. Jillian was always asking about my big-house family. I thought she would like to meet them all. And Nannie's friends, too.

"Jillian, would you like to come to Nannie's party? *If* we have it, that is," I said.

"I would love to, Karen! Thank you," said Jillian.

"Great. I will see you tomorrow," I replied.

I hugged Lulu good-bye. Then I headed for Elizabeth's car.

14

Choosing

Now, let me see. What should I choose to be? A juggler? A trapeze flyer? An acrobat? A clown? I just could not decide.

It was Monday of our last week of camp. The circus was going to be on Saturday. I had to choose one thing to do. I had to.

But I did not want to. I wanted to do everything.

"Can't I do a few things really fast?" I asked B. F. Willie.

"I am afraid not," said Mr. Willie. "You must choose one thing. You must rehearse it this week. Otherwise you will not be ready to perform on Saturday."

"Oh, all right. If I have to choose something, I choose the trapeze," I blurted out.

"Good for you, Karen. Brenda, my daughter-in-law, will help you get ready for the show," said Mr. Willie.

I did it. I chose. I do not know why I chose the trapeze. It was the first thing that popped into my head. But it would be okay. Nancy chose the trapeze. So did two other kids I liked. We would have fun.

When I got there, Jillian was helping Brenda.

"I am glad you picked the trapeze. Now we can practice together," she said.

Good. I made the right choice. I would work with Jillian. And I would be with Nancy, too.

Jillian helped me put on my harness. Then I climbed up the ladder to the platform. Brenda was already there.

"Are you ready to try a new stunt?" she asked.

"Sure," I replied.

She showed us all how to hang from the swing upside down. We each took a turn practicing.

"That looks great, Karen," called Jillian.

I did really well on the trapeze. And I had fun, too. But something was bothering me.

At the end of the day, I went to find Mr. Willie.

"I think I made a mistake," I said. "The trapeze is not for me. Can I change my mind? Can I work on, um, the high wire?"

"If it would make you happier, you can switch," said Mr. Willie. "You can join the high wire group tomorrow."

"Thank you, Mr. Willie," I said.

I breathed a sigh of relief. Then I started to worry again. High wire? Why did I say high wire?

15

Telling

When I got home, I had another big decision to make.

Tell. Don't tell. Tell. Don't tell.

Tomorrow night was Nannie's birthday party. I had to tell her about it right away. Otherwise, I could not tell her at all.

Here are the things I knew. I knew I would be in big trouble if anyone at the big house found out I had been eavesdropping. I knew that Nannie would hate being surprised. I knew that Jillian thought I should tell Nannie everything.

I decided to listen to Jillian.

Nannie was upstairs resting before dinner. I went to her room and knocked lightly on her door.

"Come in," called Nannie.

I poked my head in.

"Um, can I talk to you for a few minutes?" I asked.

"Of course. Close the door behind you," said Nannie.

"First of all, I am sorry," I said.

"What are you sorry about?" asked Nanny.

"I am sorry that I eavesdropped on you," I said. "I stood outside your door and listened to you talk on the phone. I know I will have to be punished. But do you think you could punish me without anyone knowing? Without Daddy or Elizabeth knowing?"

There. I said it. It was all very clear to me. But Nannie looked confused. So I kept on talking. I had to make her understand.

"The reason I *have* to tell you about eavesdropping is that I heard you say something important," I said. "I heard you tell your friend that you hate surprises. And the thing is, we were planning to give you a surprise party."

Nannie gasped. Her face turned pale.

"Oh, my. I really do not like surprises," she said.

"We were only planning the surprise party because we love you so much. No one would ever want to embarrass you," I explained. "But now everyone is looking forward to the party. They have so many nice things planned. They will be very upset if they cannot give you this party."

I also knew they would be very upset if they knew I was spoiling the surprise right that very minute.

"Well, thank you for telling me, Karen. I know that was not easy for you," said Nannie. "What do you think we should do?"

"I don't know. I will have to think some

more. I promise to figure out something,"
I replied.

"We should be able to think of something
between the two of us," said Nannie. "And
about your punishment. I think we can skip
that. We all make mistakes. And you did
tell me about it. But will you promise me
you will try to break that bad habit?"

I threw my arms around Nannie.

"I promise!" I said.

And I meant it.

"I Changed My Mind"

I went to camp early Tuesday morning. I wanted to get to work on the high wire. Jimmy helped me make up what I had missed.

"Yesterday we practiced turning, and walking backward," said Jimmy. "Come, I will show you how."

By the time the other kids came, I felt caught up.

Robin was in the group. (She was the one who was so scared when she started. Now she was one of the best kids on the high

74

wire.) And there were two boys. Their names were Joseph and Gregory.

"I have a tape of the music the circus band will be playing on Saturday," said Jimmy. "Today we will work on crossing the high wire in time to the music. Karen, why don't you go first. Robin will be your spotter at the net."

Jimmy turned on the tape player. The circus music made me feel like dancing right across the high wire. Oh, yes! This was the group for me!

I stepped out onto the wire with my balancing rod. I started across in time to the music.

But something across the tent caught my eye. Up and down. Up and down. Nancy was bouncing up and down on the trampoline. Gee, that looked like fun.

Whoa! I was so busy watching, I fell off the high wire.

"It is a good thing you practiced that fall this morning, Karen," said Jimmy. "Are you okay?"

"I'm okay," I said.

I did my forward tumble off the net. I landed feet first.

"Your attention should be on the high wire, not the trampoline," said Jimmy. "Will you be Robin's spotter now?"

"Sure," I replied.

I stood at the side of the net ready to help Robin when she came down from the wire.

Robin was doing a very good job walking backward in time to the music.

Out of the corner of my eye, I could see the jugglers tossing bean bags into the air. Uh-oh. Ricky dropped one. I raced to pick it up for him.

When I got back, Robin was already off the high wire and in the net.

"Karen, you were supposed to be watching Robin. Please stay with the group," said Jimmy.

"I just have to do one thing first," I said. "I will be right back."

The acrobats needed another person for

their pyramid. I raced over and climbed to the top. Ta-dah!

On the way back, I saw Lulu being led into the ring.

"Hi, Lulu!" I called. I hurried over to hug her.

I went back to the high wire and stayed there five whole minutes. But the clowns were piling into their clown car. *Honk! Honk!* I wondered if they had an extra clown nose for me.

By the end of the day, no one was very surprised when I said, "I changed my mind. I do not want to be a high wire artist after all."

"What do you want to be now?" asked B. F. Willie.

"I want to be, um, a juggler. Probably. I think," I replied.

Surprise!

Nannie and I had a secret plan. No one would know about it until the party. It was Tuesday night. The party was on!

At six o'clock, Nannie came out of her room.

"Good-bye, everyone," she said. "I am going out to dinner with a few of my bowling friends. I will not be back very late."

"Good-bye, Nannie," said Kristy.

"Have a lovely dinner," I said.

I did not even wink at Nannie. I was afraid someone might catch on if I did.

Nannie went outside and started up the Pink Clinker. (That is the name of Nannie's car.) She pulled out of the driveway. As soon as she turned the corner, Charlie called, "Okay, everyone. The coast is clear!"

We started packing up Daddy's car.

"I can't find the streamers," called Elizabeth.

"We hid them in the umbrella stand," said Kristy. "The balloons are there, too."

"Does anyone know where Nannie's birthday presents are?" asked Daddy.

"They are in my room, under my bed," I replied. "I will go get them."

When the car was loaded up, we headed to the bowling alley. We were there by a quarter to seven. A sign on the door said *Closed for Private Party*. That was our party! I felt gigundoly important.

There was a lot to do before Nannie arrived at seven-thirty.

We had to put up the decorations, set out the food and presents, and greet all the guests. Here are the people who were coming: Hannie and Nancy and their families; some friends of Nannie who were not on her bowling team; friends of Daddy and Elizabeth; Jillian and B. F. Willie.

"Five minutes to countdown," said Sam.

"Let's keep the noise down, so we don't give away the surprise," said Charlie.

It was time. I sneaked away from the rest of the group. I walked to the front of the bowling alley and waited.

When Nannie got there, I took her hand and walked inside with her, just as we had planned. I knew she felt better knowing what was coming and having me by her side.

"Surprise!!!" everyone shouted at once.

Nannie smiled. She threw up her hands and acted really surprised.

"My goodness. A surprise party! How thoughtful of you to go to all this trouble," said Nannie.

She gave me the first hug. She whispered in my ear, "Thank you, Karen."

80

One by one the guests came to wish Nannie happy birthday. When it was Jillian's turn, I could see tears in her eyes. Hmm. That was strange.

"Happy birthday, Nannie," said Jillian. "I am happy to meet you."

Oh, well. Jillian really is sweet. I guess she was very happy for Nannie. That must be why she had tears in her eyes.

I was happy for Nannie, too. By the time we sang "Happy Birthday" to her, I could tell she was having a really good time.

Whew! What a relief.

The Ringmaster

Here is the sad news: It was my last day of circus camp.

Here is the happy news: Tomorrow was our circus show.

It was going to be so much fun. Nancy was going to be on the trapeze. Hannie was riding Lulu bareback. Ricky was juggling. Natalie was going to be a clown. And I . . . I . . .

Uh-oh. I still did not know what I was going to do. I was not prepared to do anything. I had done something different every day. So I did not know any of the routines very well.

I had to find B. F. Willie. I had to talk to him.

"Mr. Willie, I don't know what to do in the circus tomorrow," I said.

"Well, maybe you could be a clown," suggested Mr. Willie. "You could make up a routine today."

I knew Mr. Willie was trying to be nice.

"Thank you," I said. "It is a good idea."

But I did not want to be a clown. A clown would not wear a hot pink spangly tutu.

I did not know what to do. I felt like crying.

Everyone was going to be at the circus. Mommy, Seth, Andrew, Daddy, and my whole big-house family. Jillian would be watching me, too. I did not want to mess up in front of them. I would be so embarrassed.

Just then, Jillian ran over.

"Grandpa!" she cried. "Todd's father just stopped by. Todd has a fever. He cannot be in the circus tomorrow. The doctor won't let him."

I knew who Todd was. He was supposed to be the ringmaster. If he could not be ringmaster, someone would have to take his place.

"Mr. Willie?" I said. "Could I be the ring-master? I know all the acts."

"You know, that is not a bad idea at all," said Mr. Willie. "You really have done everything there is to do in this circus. I do not think anyone could do a better job than you."

"Yipee!" I shouted. "Can I wear my spangly tutu?"

"The ringmaster always wears a tuxedo jacket. But I do not see why our ringmis-tress cannot wear a tutu underneath," said Mr. Willie.

Perfect. I could wear the jacket open. Then everyone would see my spangly let-ter K.

Karen Brewer, Ringmistress. Whew. I made it through another close call.

19

Karen's Big Top

"Ladies and gentlemen! Children of all ages! Welcome to the B. F. Willie Big Top!" I cried.

I looked around at all the people watching me. I started to get nervous. It felt like there were butterflies in my stomach. But somehow I just knew everything would be okay.

I looked gigundoly beautiful. I was wearing a black top hat, black tuxedo jacket, my hot pink tutu, black tights, and black ballet slippers. I checked to see that my jacket was open. I wanted to make sure everyone could see my spangly K.

The next thing I knew, I heard a drumroll from the band. Suddenly my butterflies were gone. I was ready to introduce the first act.

"Please cast your eyes upward to the flying trapeze. See three fearless campers perform amazing feats of daring!" I said.

Nancy and her partners took turns swinging from the flying trapeze. They looked very brave. (For a minute I wished I were up there too. But only for a minute. I was happy being ringmistress.)

When they finished, horns blew and cymbals crashed. The audience clapped and cheered. Then there was another drumroll. (The drumroll meant I was supposed to announce the next act.)

"Now you will see our amazing juggling team. Let's hear it for the jugglers!" I said.

They walked to the center of the ring. My

husband, Ricky, was at the front of the line. The jugglers had on matching red capes, with black shirts, leotards, and sneakers.

They each sent three beanbags flying up in the air. Then they juggled the nine bags back and forth between them.

"Ah . . . ah . . . ah . . . choo!" sneezed Ricky.

Oh, no. My very own husband missed the bean bag. That set everyone off. Nine beanbags came sailing down to the ground.

"Gesundheit, Mr. Juggler. You get A for effort," I said. "Let's hear it for our jugglers."

The crowd went wild. The band played "All Around the Mulberry Bush." Then came the drumroll.

"Get your funnybones ready, everyone. Here come the B. F. Willie clowns!" I called.

Honk! Honk! Natalie came scooting out, honking her nose and pulling up her socks.

(Her socks really do droop all the time.) A clown car rolled up and six clowns climbed out. Natalie jumped in the car and drove away. The other clowns chased her around and around the circus ring. *Honk! Honk!*

"Hip, hip, hooray for the B. F. Willie clowns," I said.

I waited for the drumroll. Then I introduced the next act.

"Here comes Hannie Papadakis, riding bareback on the beautiful pony, Lulu!" I called.

Hannie looked like a real and true circus star. She had on a white leotard with gold sequins. She wore a band around her forehead with a big feather stuck in the front. (I gave Hannie the feather I found. I decided I did not need a feather for my tutu after all.)

Hannie rode Lulu around and around the ring. She even turned around and rode backward. Then she galloped away.

"Bravo! Bravo for Hannie Papadakis!" I cried.

I introduced all the acts in the circus. I did not make one mistake. I loved every minute of it.

And do you know what? At the end of the circus the audience stood up and clapped for *me*.

Thank you! Thank you! Thank you!

20

So Long

"Karen, honey, you were terrific," said Mommy.

"We were all so proud of you," said Daddy.

"How about a trip to the Rosebud Cafe for an ice-cream celebration?" suggested Elizabeth.

"All right!" I said. "Can Jillian come with us?"

"Thanks, Karen," said Jillian. "But I have to stay here. We're going to be packing up and hitting the road again."

92

A minute ago I was so happy. But now I was sad. I forgot that when camp was over, the B. F. Willie Big Top was leaving town. That meant that Jillian was leaving town. She would not be back for a whole year. It was time to say good-bye to my friend.

"Um, can I talk to Jillian? Alone? I will not be very long," I said to my family.

"You go ahead. We will wait here for you," said Elizabeth.

Jillian and I walked out back where it was quiet. We sat on the bale of hay.

"The circus is leaving tomorrow," said Jillian. "We never stay anywhere for very long. Our month in Stoneybrook is our longest stop."

"I guess it is exciting going to new places all the time. Right?" I asked.

"Sure. It is exciting performing in a circus and seeing new places. But I get pretty tired of it sometimes. I wish I could live in one place the way you do," said Jillian.

"I guess I am pretty lucky," I said. "I

have to go back and forth between two houses. But they are not very far away. And I see my same friends all the time."

"Every time I make a new friend, I know I am going to have to say good-bye," said Jillian. "But I hardly ever make new friends because we are never in one place long enough. I am really glad I made friends with you, Karen."

Jillian had tears in her eyes again. Just the way she had at Nannie's party. I felt my eyes filling up, too.

"You really will come back next summer, won't you?" I asked.

"I sure will. And I will write to you while I am gone. I will send you funny post-cards from everywhere I go. Will you write back?" asked Jillian.

"I sure will," I said. "I have to go see my family now. So long, Jillian."

"So long, Karen."

Jillian and I gave each other big hugs. Then we walked inside. Jillian went off to start packing.

I went off to have an ice-cream celebration. Then I was going home to pack, too.

July at the big house was fun. Now I was looking forward to August at the little house.

"I really am lucky," I thought. "I really and truly am."

About the Author

ANN M. MARTIN lives in New York City and loves animals, especially cats. She has two cats of her own, Mouse and Rosie.

Other books by Ann M. Martin that you might enjoy are *Stage Fright*; *Me and Katie (the Pest)*; and the books in *The Baby-sitters Club* series.

Ann likes ice cream and *I Love Lucy*. And she has her own little sister, whose name is Jane.

Little Sister

Don't miss #52

KAREN'S MERMAID

I stared at the note. I had never felt so surprised. A mermaid named Neptuna was writing to me? And she wanted me to be her friend? That was so exciting.

And yet . . . hadn't I made up the story about seeing a mermaid? Hadn't I made it up for Margo?

I thought for a moment. Maybe not. Maybe I thought up the story about the mermaid because I really had seen one, just a little glimpse of one out of the corner of my eye.

I decided I better keep Neptuna a secret from everyone.

Little Sister™

by Ann M. Martin, author of *The Baby-sitters Club*®

More Titles... ➡

888888888888888888888888888888888888

The Baby-sitters Little Sister titles continued...

☐ MQ44825-0	#29	Karen's Cartwheel	$2.75
☐ MQ45645-8	#30	Karen's Kittens	$2.75
☐ MQ45646-6	#31	Karen's Bully	$2.95
☐ MQ45647-4	#32	Karen's Pumpkin Patch	$2.95
☐ MQ45648-2	#33	Karen's Secret	$2.95
☐ MQ45650-4	#34	Karen's Snow Day	$2.95
☐ MQ45652-0	#35	Karen's Doll Hospital	$2.95
☐ MQ45651-2	#36	Karen's New Friend	$2.95
☐ MQ45653-9	#37	Karen's Tuba	$2.95
☐ MQ45655-5	#38	Karen's Big Lie	$2.95
☐ MQ45654-7	#39	Karen's Wedding	$2.95
☐ MQ47040-X	#40	Karen's Newspaper	$2.95
☐ MQ47041-8	#41	Karen's School	$2.95
☐ MQ47042-6	#42	Karen's Pizza Party	$2.95
☐ MQ46912-6	#43	Karen's Toothache	$2.95
☐ MQ47043-4	#44	Karen's Big Weekend	$2.95
☐ MQ47044-2	#45	Karen's Twin	$2.95
☐ MQ47045-0	#46	Karen's Baby-sitter	$2.95
☐ MQ43647-3		Karen's Wish Super Special #1	$2.95
☐ MQ44834-X		Karen's Plane Trip Super Special #2	$3.25
☐ MQ44827-7		Karen's Mystery Super Special #3	$2.95
☐ MQ45644-X		Karen's Three Musketeers Super Special #4	$2.95
☐ MQ45649-0		Karen's Baby Super Special #5	$3.25
☐ MQ46911-8		Karen's Campout Super Special #6	$3.25

Available wherever you buy books, or use this order form.

Scholastic Inc., P.O. Box 7502, 2931 E. McCarty Street, Jefferson City, MO 65102
Please send me the books I have checked above. I am enclosing $ _____
(please add $2.00 to cover shipping and handling). Send check or money order - no cash
or C.O.Ds please.

Name _____ Birthdate _____

Address _____

City _____ State/Zip _____
Please allow four to six weeks for delivery. Offer good in U.S.A. only. Sorry, mail orders are not
available to residents to Canada. Prices subject to change.   BLS793

888888888888888888888888888888888888

Create Your Own Mystery Stories!

MYSTERY GAME!

WHO: Boyfriend **WHY:** Romance
WHAT: Phone Call **WHERE:** Dance

Use the special Mystery Case card to pick WHO did it, WHAT was involved, WHY it happened and WHERE it happened. Then dial secret words on your Mystery Wheels to add to the story! Travel around the special Stoneybrook map gameboard to uncover your friends' secret word clues! Finish four baby-sitting jobs and find out all the words to win. Then have everyone join in to tell the story!